DRAWING DIPLODOCUS
AND OTHER PLANT-EATING DINOSAURS

STEVE BEAUMONT

PowerKiDS
press.

New York

Published in 2010 by The Rosen Publishing Group, Inc.
29 East 21st Street, New York, NY 10010

Copyright © 2010 Arcturus Publishing Ltd

Artwork and text: Steve Beaumont
Editor (Arcturus): Carron Brown
Designer: Steve Flight

Library of Congress Cataloging-in-Publication Data

Beaumont, Steve.
  Drawing Diplodocus and other plant-eating dinosaurs / Steve Beaumont. —
1st ed.
      p. cm. — (Drawing dinosaurs)
  Includes index.
  ISBN 978-1-61531-902-2 (library binding) — ISBN 978-1-4488-0424-5 (pbk.) —
ISBN 978-1-4488-0425-2 (6-pack)
  1. Dinosaurs in art—Juvenile literature. 2. Drawing—Technique—Juvenile literature.
  3. Diplodocus—Juvenile literature. I. Title.
  NC780.5.B39 2010
  743.6—dc22
                                        2009033274

Printed in China

CPSIA compliance information: Batch #AW0102PK : For further information contact Rosen Publishing, New York, New York at 1-800-237-9932

CONTENTS

"Dinosaurs"... the word conjures up all kinds of powerful and exciting images. From the huge swooping neck of Diplodocus to the large claws of Iguanodon and the duck-billed, crested Parasaurolophus—dinosaurs came in all shapes and sizes.

These amazing creatures ruled Earth for over 160 million years until, suddenly, they all died out. No one has ever seen a living, moving, roaring dinosaur, but thanks to the research of paleontologists, who piece together dinosaur fossils, we now have a pretty good idea what many of them looked like.

Some were as big as huge buildings, others had enormous teeth, scaly skin, horns, claws, and body armor. Dinosaurs have played starring roles in books, on television, and in blockbuster movies and now it's time for them to take center stage on your drawing pad!

In this book we've chosen three incredible plant-eating dinosaurs for you to learn how to draw. We've also included a dinosaur landscape for you to sketch, so you can really set the prehistoric scene for your drawings.

You'll find advice on the essential drawing tools you'll need to get started, tips on how to get the best results from your drawings, and easy-to-follow step-by-step instructions showing you how to draw each dinosaur. So, it's time to bring these extinct monsters back to life—let's draw some dinosaurs!

DRAWING TOOLS

Let's start with the essential drawing tools you'll need to create awesome illustrations. Build up your collection as your drawing skills improve.

LAYOUT PAPER

Artists, both as professionals and as students, rarely produce their first practice sketches on their best quality art paper. It's a good idea to buy some inexpensive plain letter-size paper from a stationery store for all of your practice sketches. Buy the least expensive kind.

Most professional illustrators use cheaper paper for basic layouts and practice sketches before they get to the more serious task of producing a masterpiece on more costly material.

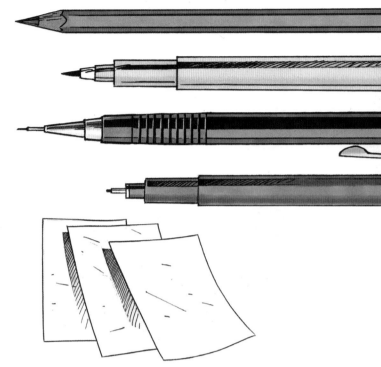

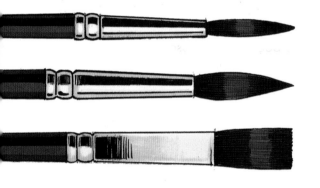

HEAVY DRAWING PAPER

This paper is ideal for your final version. You don't have to buy the most expensive brand—most decent arts and crafts stores will stock their own brand or another lower-priced brand and unless you're thinking of turning professional, these will work fine.

WATERCOLOR PAPER

This paper is made from 100 percent cotton and is much higher quality than wood-based papers. Most arts and crafts stores will stock a large range of weights and sizes—140 pounds per ream (300 g/sq m) will be fine.

LINE ART PAPER

If you want to practice black and white ink drawing, line art paper enables you to produce a nice clear crisp line. You'll get better results than you would on heavier paper as it has a much smoother surface.

PENCILS

It's best not to cut corners on quality here. Get a good range of graphite (lead) pencils ranging from soft (#1) to hard (#4).

Hard lead lasts longer and leaves less graphite on the paper. Soft lead leaves more lead on the paper and wears down more quickly. Every artist has his personal preference, but #2.5 pencils are a good medium grade to start out with until you find your own favorite.

Spend some time drawing with each grade of pencil and get used to their different qualities. Another good product to try is the clutch, or mechanical pencil. These are available in a range of lead thicknesses, 0.5mm being a good medium size. These pencils are very good for fine detail work.

PENS

There is a large range of good quality pens on the market and all will do a decent job of inking. It's important to experiment with a range of different pens to determine which you find most comfortable to work with.

You may find that you end up using a combination of pens to produce your finished piece of artwork. Remember to use a pen that has waterproof ink if you want to color your illustration with a watercolor or ink wash.

It's a good idea to use one of these—there's nothing worse than having your nicely inked drawing ruined by an accidental drop of water!

BRUSHES

Some artists like to use a fine brush for inking linework. This takes a bit more practice and patience to master, but the results can be very satisfying. If you want to try your hand at brushwork, you will definitely need to get some good-quality sable brushes.

ERASER

There are three main types of erasers: rubber, plastic, and putty. Try all three to see which kind you prefer.

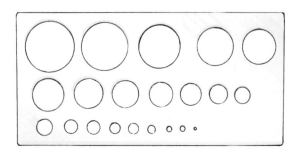

PANTONE MARKERS

These are very versatile pens and with practice can give pleasing results.

INKS

With the rise of computers and digital illustration, materials such as inks have become a bit obscure, so you may have to look harder for these, but most good arts and crafts stores should stock them.

WATERCOLORS AND GOUACHE

Most art stores will stock a wide range of these products, from professional to student quality.

CIRCLE TEMPLATE

This is very useful for drawing small circles.

FRENCH CURVES

These are available in a few shapes and sizes and are useful for drawing curves.

BUILDING DINOSAURS

Notice how a simple oval shape forms the body of these three dinosaurs (figs.1, 2, and 3). Even though they are all very differently shaped, an oval forms the body of each one perfectly.

Fig. 4 shows how a dinosaur can be constructed using all these basic shapes. Cylinders are used for its legs and arms, an oval shape forms its body, and a smaller egg shape is used for its head.

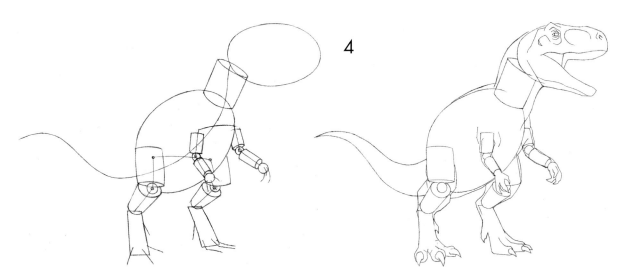

DRAWING FEET

Meat-eating dinosaurs such as T. rex have feet that resemble those of a large bird, but the feet of bulkier plant-eating dinosaurs such as Diplodocus and Triceratops look very different. See the columns below to learn how to construct T. rex and Diplodocus feet.

T. REX FOOT   **DIPLODOCUS FOOT**

STEP 1

First draw your basic shapes. T. rex (left) is mainly constructed using a rectangle, with lines for the toes. For the flatter Diplodocus foot (right), use a semicircle and a cylinder.

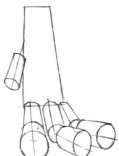
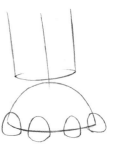

STEP 2

Use two cylinders for each of T. rex's toes. The little toe that sits higher up on the foot only needs one. With Diplodocus's feet, add circular shapes to form the toenails.

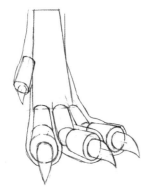

STEP 3
Now flesh out the feet adding skin and claws.

STEP 4
Erase all of your construction shapes. Add detail to the skin and finally some shading to bring depth to the drawing. There you have it— two very different dinosaur feet!

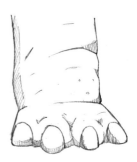

DIPLODOCUS

DINO FACT FILE
Diplodocus was a plant-loving gentle giant. It was one of the largest land animals ever to have existed, measuring about 90 feet (27 m) in length—that's the same as three buses! Its nostrils were on top of its head and its teeth were like pegs. "Diplodocus" means "double beam," referring to its long neck and powerful tail, which it swung like a whip to defend itself from predators.

STEP 1
Start by drawing the basic stick figure.

STEP 2
Add the basic construction shapes. Use cylinders to build up the neck and tail. Its legs and feet are similar to those of an elephant.

STEP 3
Add the skin by drawing around the shapes. Start to remove some of your stick figure lines. Then add the facial features.

STEP 4
Remove all the construction shapes and start finalizing your pencil drawing. Add claws and texture to the skin. Leave areas you intend to shade blank. For added interest, we've shown the Diplodocus munching on some fern leaves.

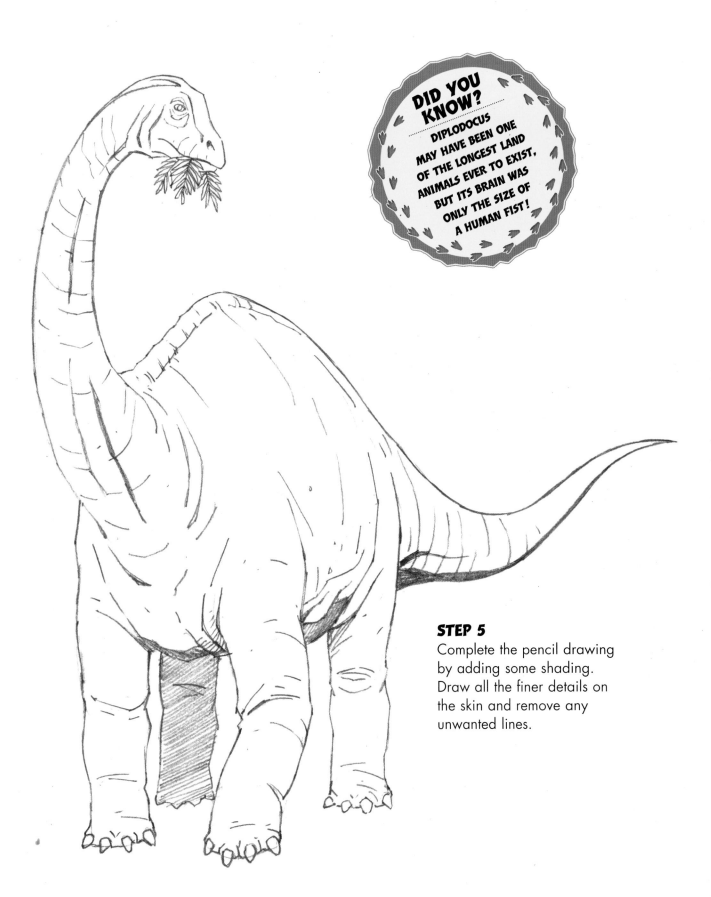

DID YOU KNOW?

DIPLODOCUS MAY HAVE BEEN ONE OF THE LONGEST LAND ANIMALS EVER TO EXIST, BUT ITS BRAIN WAS ONLY THE SIZE OF A HUMAN FIST!

STEP 5

Complete the pencil drawing by adding some shading. Draw all the finer details on the skin and remove any unwanted lines.

STEP 6

Now ink over the pencil lines. Use solid black ink for the shaded areas.

STEP 7

Use a pale sand color for the base and go over this with a very pale olive green. Next apply a pale gray on top of the olive. Finish off by using a dark gray on the claws and to shade in any folds in the skin. Color the bunch of leaves in a bright green.

IGUANODON

DINO FACT FILE

Iguanodon's most distinctive features were its large thumb spikes. These claws were possibly used for defense against predators or digging up plants to eat. It was one of the first dinosaurs to be discovered and was later named Iguanodon or "iguana tooth." Its pointed beak was completely toothless and all its teeth were in its cheeks. It was able to run on two legs or walk on all fours.

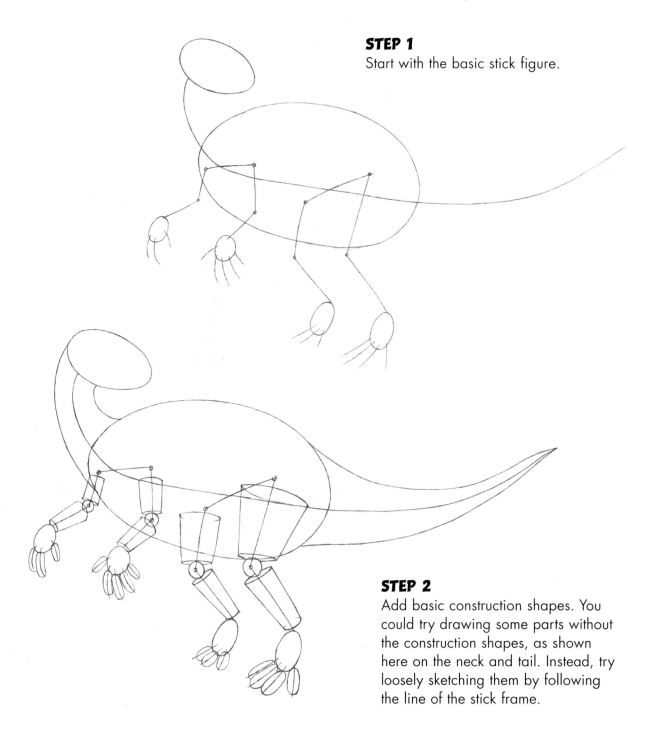

STEP 1
Start with the basic stick figure.

STEP 2
Add basic construction shapes. You could try drawing some parts without the construction shapes, as shown here on the neck and tail. Instead, try loosely sketching them by following the line of the stick frame.

STEP 3

Draw the skin around the basic shapes. Add facial features and claws and remove your stick figure lines.

STEP 4

Add some wrinkles and creases to the skin on the neck, arms, legs, tail, and face. Then remove all of your construction shapes.

STEP 5

Now add shading to the final pencil drawing and clean up any unwanted lines.

STEP 6
Ink over the pencil drawing.
Develop the skin texture as
you do so.

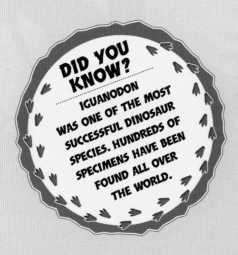

DID YOU KNOW?

IGUANODON WAS ONE OF THE MOST SUCCESSFUL DINOSAUR SPECIES. HUNDREDS OF SPECIMENS HAVE BEEN FOUND ALL OVER THE WORLD.

STEP 7

Start to color the Iguanodon using a sand-colored base. Add a pale olive green down its back and tail and around its head, creating a textured effect. Use a midrange gray to add shading around the creases and folds in the skin and on the claws.

PARASAUROLOPHUS

DINO FACT FILE

Parasaurolophus was a sturdy, duck-billed dinosaur whose distinguishing feature was a hollow, bony crest on its head. It had pebble-like scales and, like Iguanodon, a toothless beak and cheek teeth. Its crest is believed to have enhanced its sense of smell, as its nostrils ran all the way up it and back down in four tubes. This would have helped its survival as it had no natural defenses.

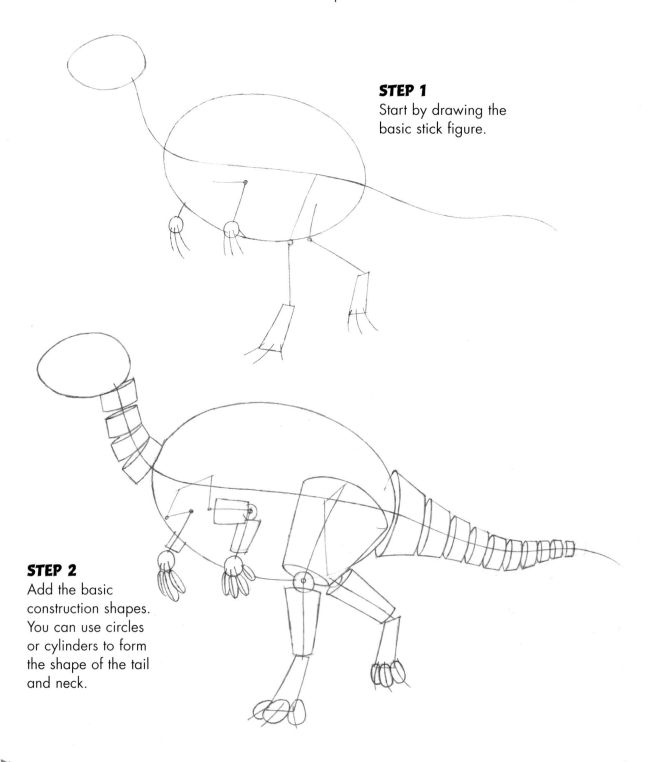

STEP 1
Start by drawing the basic stick figure.

STEP 2
Add the basic construction shapes. You can use circles or cylinders to form the shape of the tail and neck.

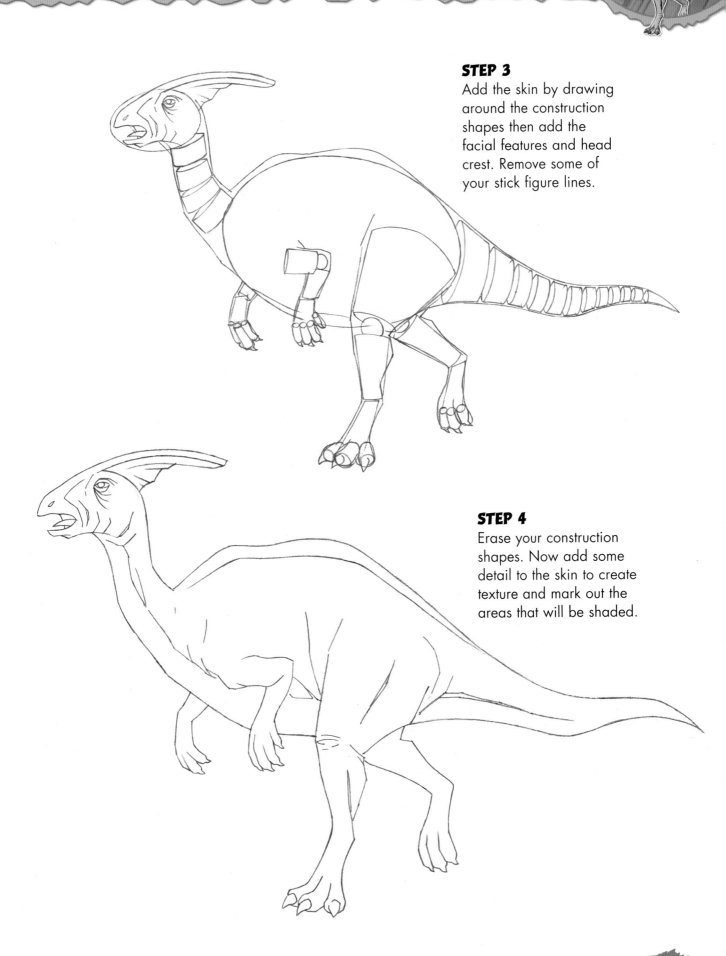

STEP 3

Add the skin by drawing around the construction shapes then add the facial features and head crest. Remove some of your stick figure lines.

STEP 4

Erase your construction shapes. Now add some detail to the skin to create texture and mark out the areas that will be shaded.

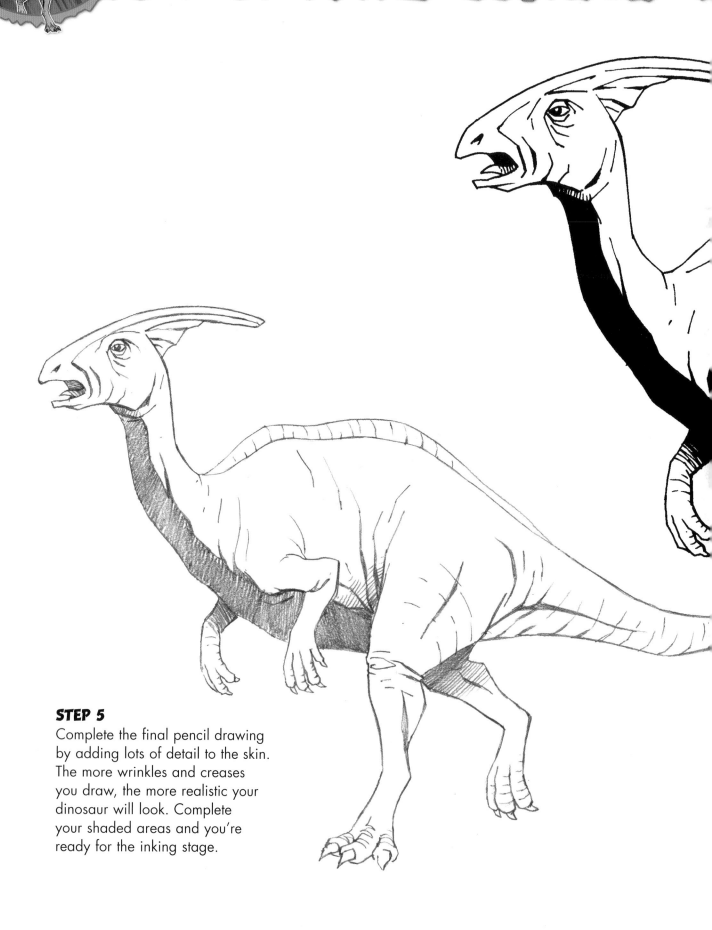

STEP 5

Complete the final pencil drawing
by adding lots of detail to the skin.
The more wrinkles and creases
you draw, the more realistic your
dinosaur will look. Complete
your shaded areas and you're
ready for the inking stage.

STEP 6
Once you're finished with
your pencil drawing, go
over it in ink, using solid
blocks of black ink for
the shaded areas.

STEP 7

Color the Parasaurolophus by starting with a sand-colored base. Then use a peach color on its back, neck, tail, and face. Leave the top half of the crest in the sandy base color. Finish off by using a midrange pink on top of the peach color. A slightly patchy appearance will give the skin a textured effect.

DID YOU KNOW?

SCIENTISTS THINK PARASAUROLOPHUS MIGHT HAVE USED ITS HOLLOW CREST TO PRODUCE A LOUD NOISE THAT SOUNDED LIKE A FOGHORN!

CREATING A SCENE

LANDSCAPE FEATURING DIPLODOCUS

Diplodocus lived about 155 million years ago. This was the time of the first flying dinosaurs and the giant plant eaters, which grazed in herds on a variety of plants across the prehistoric landscape. Diplodocus roamed the plains and valleys of North America, where it ate ferns and leaves.

STEP 1 Draw the horizon line one-third up the page. Sketch in a forested area of palm trees among a cluster of ferns over the right half of the scene, and a palm tree to the left. Draw the stick figure for a Diplodocus.

STEP 2 Construct the Diplodocus (see pages 9–13 for the step-by-step guide).
Next, draw some ferns in the foreground and develop the leaf detail on the trees.

STEP 3 Draw a line of bushy ferns above the horizon line and add clouds in the sky.
Add facial features to the Diplodocus and add more definition to the legs.

STEP 4 Complete the pencil drawing by adding shading to create areas of black and all your final details to the dinosaur and scenery.

STEP 5 Finally, color your prehistoric landscape. You could experiment with other colors to create different effects.

GLOSSARY

amazing (uh-MAYZ-ing) Wonderful.

crested (KREST-ed) Having a head decoration.

cylinders (SIH-len-derz) Shapes with straight sides and circular ends of equal size.

facial (FAY-shul) Of the face.

gouache (GWAHSH) A mixture of nontransparent watercolor paint and gum.

mechanical pencil (mih-KA-nih-kul PENT-sul) A pencil with replaceable lead that may be advanced as needed.

research (rih-SERCH) Careful study.

sable brushes (SAY-bel BRUSH-ez) Artists' brushes made with the hairs of a sable, a small mammal from northern Asia.

stick figure (STIK FIH-gyur) A simple drawing of a creature with single lines for the head, neck, body, legs, and tail.

watercolor (WAH-ter-kuh-ler) Paint made by mixing pigments (substances that give something its color) with water.

INDEX

WEB SITES

Due to the changing nature of Internet links, PowerKids Press has developed an online list of Web sites related to the subject of this book. This site is updated regularly. Please use this link to access the list:
www.powerkidslinks.com/ddino/diplodocus/